For Carol Morrissey Greiner, who played dress-up with me
—T. deP.

For Mia Rose & Emmett & Joey—welcome to the adventure!
—J. L.

SIMON & SCHUSTER BOOKS FOR YOUNG READERS
An imprint of Simon & Schuster Children's Publishing Division
1230 Avenue of the Americas, New York, New York 10020
Text copyright © 2016 by Tomie dePaola and Jim Lewis
Illustrations copyright © 2016 by Tomie dePaola
All rights reserved, including the right of reproduction in whole or in part in any form.
SIMON & SCHUSTER BOOKS FOR YOUNG READERS is a trademark of Simon & Schuster, Inc.
For information about special discounts for bulk purchases, please contact
Simon & Schuster Special Sales at 1-866-506-1949 or business@simonandschuster.com.
The Simon & Schuster Speakers Bureau can bring authors to your live event.
For more information or to book an event, contact the Simon & Schuster Speakers Bureau
at 1-866-248-3049 or visit our website at www.simonspeakers.com.
Book design by Laurent Linn
The text for this book is set in Minister Std.
The illustrations for this book are rendered in acrylics with colored pencil
on 150lb Fabriano Cold Press 100% rag watercolor paper.
Manufactured in China
1215 SCP
2 4 6 8 10 9 7 5 3 1
Library of Congress Cataloging-in-Publication Data
DePaola, Tomie, 1934–
Andy & Sandy's anything adventure / Tomie dePaola, with Jim Lewis. — First edition.
pages cm
Summary: "Andy is small. Sandy is tall. Andy is quiet. Sandy is LOUD. When these two
opposites-attract best friends play dress-up, anything can happen"— Provided by publisher.
ISBN 978-1-4814-4157-5 (hardcover) — ISBN 978-1-4814-4158-2 (ebook)
[1. Best friends—Fiction. 2. Friendship—Fiction. 3. English language—Synonyms and
antonyms—Fiction.] I. Lewis, Jim, 1955– II. Title. III. Title: Andy and Sandy's anything
adventure.
PZ7.D439Ak 2016
[E]—dc23
2015003164

Andy & Sandy's Anything Adventure

Tomie dePaola
COWRITTEN WITH Jim Lewis

SIMON & SCHUSTER BOOKS FOR YOUNG READERS

New York   London   Toronto   Sydney   New Delhi

Hi, Andy!

Hi, Sandy!

Do you want
to play checkers?

Do you want
to play dinosaurs?

I am a cowgirl
riding my horse!

I am a pirate
sailing the seven seas!

I am a bumblebee
buzzing all around!

What can we be now?

I have another idea.

Me too.

I am you!

And I am you!

And together we
are always friends.

Wicked
Witch
Hat

duck mask
and
feet

Wicked Witch mask
and wig

wicked
witch
dress

broom

cauldron

shoes

Drawings by Sandy